Fight for the Throne

THE CHRONICLES OF
NARNIA
PRINCE CASPIAN

Fight for
the Throne

Adapted by J. E. Bright
Based on the screenplay by Andrew Adamson &
Christopher Markus & Stephen McFeely
Based on the book by C. S. Lewis
Directed by Andrew Adamson

HarperEntertainment
An Imprint of HarperCollinsPublishers

Prince Caspian: Fight for the Throne
Copyright © 2008 by C.S. Lewis Pte. Ltd.
Art/illustration © 2008 Disney Enterprises, Inc. and Walden Media, LLC.
Printed in the United States of America.

Library of Congress catalog card number: 2007937698
ISBN 978-0-06-123158-2

Typography by Neo9 Design, Inc.
❖
First Edition

Fight for the Throne

Prologue

Years ago, four children discovered a magical land called Narnia. With help from the Great Lion Aslan, the Creator of Narnia, the Pevensies raised an army of magical creatures. They battled the evil White Witch and her ruthless minions. Aslan sacrificed himself to overthrow the Witch, but he came back to life and returned to the Pevensies through a Deep Magic. The White Witch was defeated, and the Pevensies were crowned Kings and Queens. They ruled in peace until the day they returned to their own world. They left a magical horn in Narnia, one that could call them back at any time if their help was needed.

Now Narnia is ruled by King Miraz. A race of Men called Telmarines invaded the forest, killing so many Narnians that they are now believed to be extinct. Aslan, too, has not been seen in centuries. But the few remaining Narnians are still hiding, waiting for Aslan's return, and for the return of the Kings and Queens. They are waiting for someone to come sound the horn and lead them to freedom.

Chapter 1

In my bedchamber in my uncle's castle, Professor Cornelius woke me before dawn. "Five more minutes," I begged sleepily.

Cornelius shook his head. "Come, we must hurry." He yanked me from bed and hustled me toward the wardrobe. Pushing aside the hanging cloaks, Cornelius slid open a secret panel, revealing stairs. "Your aunt has given birth to a son," my tutor explained.

While that sounded like good news, it wasn't. My uncle, Lord Miraz, ruled Narnia because I was too young to wear the

crown. Now his son could be made the royal heir instead of me . . . but only if I were dead. My life was in great danger.

I followed Cornelius into the wardrobe and closed it behind me just as soldiers stormed into my bedchamber. Through a crack in the wardrobe door, I saw General Glozelle give an order. His men raised their crossbows . . . and loosed their quarrels straight into my bed.

I stifled a scream as the crossbow bolts hit where I had been sleeping moments before.

They would have killed me!

Cornelius pulled me into the secret passageway and down the stairs. We crept past guards into the armory, where my small, quiet tutor outfitted me with armor, a sword and a cloak. Then we kept to the shadows until we reached the stable. My black horse, Destrier, was saddled and ready.

"You must make for the wood," Cornelius said as I mounted. "They won't follow you there." He handed me a package wrapped in cloth. "It has taken me many years to find this," he explained. "Do not use it except at your greatest need."

I held the package against my chest. "Will I ever see you again?" I whispered.

Cornelius smiled fondly. "I hope so, my Prince." He glanced out the stable door. "Everything you know is about to change."

A guard shouted nearby, and we heard the thump of boots running toward us.

Cornelius slapped my horse's rump. "Now go!" he hissed.

I gripped the reins as Destrier galloped toward the gate.

Beyond the stone arch, the drawbridge was lowered, but guards stood on either side of the exit. They blocked my path. Destrier easily sidestepped one, and I gave the other a whack on his helmet with the butt of my sword.

A squad of soldiers on horseback stampeded out of the gate, chasing me, so I hurried Destrier through the cobbled streets of the town. Beyond the town were farms and plains. The soldiers began to catch up as we raced across the fields, heading for the forest.

At the tree line, I remembered the terrifying stories I'd been told. Dangerous beasts lived within the wood, mythical monsters like Centaurs and Minotaurs and giant Talking Lions. I knew these were just stories told to frighten children, but I still shuddered as Destrier jumped into the forest.

Because of those same stories, the soldiers hesitated at the forest's edge . . . until General Glozelle ordered them to keep chasing me.

Destrier dashed through the dense wood, as branches lashed my face. I lowered my body against my horse's back, struggling to hold on. Destrier stumbled as we lurched across a rushing stream, but we made it across.

After a rush down a sheer slope, I no longer heard the soldiers behind me. I turned around to check if I could still see them.

Nothing. We'd lost them. I smiled and turned back around.

Wham! A thick branch hit my forehead. I flew out of the saddle and slammed into the underbrush. Startled, Destrier galloped off into the distance.

My head throbbed where I'd been whacked.

When things came into focus, I saw a small door open in the trunk of a nearby tree. Out of the doorway, a black-haired Dwarf glared at me. I scrambled backward as two more creatures appeared—a red-haired Dwarf and some kind of tall, furry beast.

"He's seen us," the black-haired Dwarf growled.

Terrified, I fumbled for Cornelius's package. The burlap wrapper opened. A small ivory horn fell to the ground, gleaming in the moonlight.

Both Dwarfs gaped at the horn. Then we all stiffened, hearing the sound of hooves pounding toward us. Glozelle's soldiers were back!

The red-haired Dwarf unsheathed a dagger. "Take care of him!" he ordered, and then headed toward the sound of the soldiers.

I lunged for the horn.

"No!" the black-haired Dwarf hollered, but I'd already grabbed the horn. I blew into it, blasting out an eerie, lingering note.

The Dwarf struck my head with his dagger hilt.

The call of the horn echoed throughout the forest as I lost consciousness.

Chapter 2

I awoke in a dank room that had roots crisscrossing its low ceiling. When I reached up to touch my aching head, I felt a bandage. Stranger still, someone had tucked me into bed with a blanket.

"Trufflehunter, I told you to get rid of him," a voice in the next room complained.

"No," Trufflehunter argued, "you said to *take care* of him, Nikabrik. We can't kill him now. I just bandaged his head."

My eyes widened as a giant Badger walked into the room on his hind legs, carrying a tray of food.

"It would be like murdering a guest," the Badger said.

He could *talk*! Right behind him was the black-haired Dwarf who had knocked me out. I leaped out of bed toward the door, but Nikabrik drew his dagger and blocked my exit. I grabbed a hot poker from the fireplace to protect myself.

I lowered the poker. "What *are* you?" I asked the Badger.

"You'd think you'd know a Badger when you saw one," Trufflehunter said.

"No," I replied, "I mean . . . you're Narnians. You're supposed to be extinct."

"Sorry to disappoint you," said Nikabrik. He groaned as Trufflehunter placed a bowl of soup in front of me. "When did we open a boarding house for Telmarine soldiers?"

The soup smelled wonderful. "I'm not a soldier," I said. "I'm Prince Caspian. The tenth." As I ate, they asked me what I was doing out of the castle. I explained that I had run away because my uncle had stolen the throne for his infant son. Miraz wanted to kill me so his son would become the heir to the kingdom.

"At least we won't have to kill you ourselves," added Nikabrik.

I drained the last of the soup. "You're right," I said. "My uncle won't stop until I'm dead."

"But you can't leave," said Trufflehunter. "You're meant to save us." He held up the ivory horn. "It is said that whoever blows this will call back the Ancient Kings and Queens . . . and lead us to freedom."

I strode through the den to the front door. "I hope they get here soon," I said, squeezing my way outside, "before this wood is full of Telmarine soldiers."

For the next few hours, the two Narnians followed me through the forest. Although Nikabrik was still cross, Trufflehunter tried to convince me to help them. He explained that the wood was full of Narnians—the creatures I'd thought were myths. They were desperate for a leader. But I was just an orphaned prince—the last person they should ask for help.

When we were deep in a field of waist-high ferns, Trufflehunter sniffed the air, his face full of fear. "Humans!" he hissed. "Run!"

A squad of Telmarine soldiers launched arrows at us. We

ran, but got only a little way through the ferns before an arrow hit Trufflehunter's leg. The Badger collapsed.

Trufflehunter handed me the horn. "Take it," he gasped. "It's more important than I am! Go!"

I took the horn, but then I heaved the Badger onto my shoulder and stumbled toward the wood. I couldn't just leave him there.

Meanwhile, something was attacking the soldiers in the ferns. One by one, they dropped out of view. I stopped at the forest's edge and eased Trufflehunter down next to Nikabrik, watching the field rustle in my direction. I drew my sword.

A fast blur darted out of the ferns, knocking me onto my back and disarming me. I peered up at the creature on my chest and met the fierce eyes of a two-foot-tall Mouse. "Reach for your sword," the Mouse ordered, holding a sharp rapier to my throat.

"Reepicheep!" Trufflehunter yelled. "Stay your blade! He's the one who blew the horn!"

I raised the horn, and Reepicheep lowered his rapier.

"Let him bring it forward," a deep voice called from the wood. It came from a magnificent half-man half-horse

creature, flanked by smaller Centaurs. "He is the reason we've gathered."

We followed the Centaurs into the forest, to a hidden clearing where hundreds of Narnians had assembled. I was amazed to see the creatures I thought were merely fantasy—Fauns, Satyrs, Gryphons and Giants. None of them were happy to see me. Many yelled insults, blaming me as a Telmarine for stealing their homes and freedom for centuries.

"This boy is a Son of Adam," Trufflehunter argued with the angry crowd. "Narnia has never been right except when a Son of Adam was King."

"He's a Telmarine!" Nikabrik shot back. "Why would we want him?"

"Because I can help you," I said. All the Narnians stared at me. "The Telmarine throne is rightfully mine. Help me claim it, and I can bring peace between us."

"It is true," the older Centaur added. "This Son of Adam has come forth to offer us back our freedom."

I nodded gratefully at him. "You have numbers and strength that we Telmarines never imagined," I continued, holding the horn up in the air. "Together we have a chance

to take back what is ours. We need to be ready for the arrival of the Kings and Queens of old. We need to find as many soldiers and weapons as possible. I'm sure they'll be here soon."

At least, I hoped so.

Chapter 3

We began training at dawn. Near the edge of the Narnian camp, I showed a group of Minotaurs how to hold a sword properly. We all stopped when we heard human voices coming from a grove of silver birches.

I spotted a young soldier and charged at him with my blade drawn. The soldier blocked my blow, but I pressed forward, surprised at his skill. He parried, knocking the sword from my hand, and backed me up against a tree. When the soldier swung his sword, I ducked, and his blade lodged

in the tree trunk. I knocked him down and pulled his sword free. He picked up a rock to defend himself.

"Stop!" a little girl cried. She stood in front of a large group of Narnians. They had surrounded us, their weapons drawn.

The young soldier peered at me. "Prince Caspian?" he asked.

"Yes?" I replied, confused. I glanced down at the soldier's sword in my hand. It looked strangely familiar.

"Peter!" an older girl shouted, running in from the grove. She was followed by a younger boy . . . and the red-haired Dwarf from my first night in the wood.

"*High King* Peter?" I gasped.

He tossed the rock aside. "I believe you called?"

I looked around at the group, realizing who they all were. The cute little girl was Queen Lucy. The frowning younger boy was King Edmund. The pretty teenage girl was High Queen Susan. "But . . . I thought you'd be older," I stammered.

Peter shrugged and turned to face the crowd. "Narnians, we're going to need every sword we can get!" he announced.

I smiled, offering Peter's sword back to him. "Then you'll probably be wanting yours."

After the Kings and Queens greeted the group of Narnians, I led them through the forest toward a massive tree-covered hill. At the base of the hill, hidden behind ancient ruins, a steep ramp led deep into the earth. This was Aslan's How, where we had set up our military headquarters.

When the sentries saw us emerge from the wood, they sounded the horns. The Centaurs lined up along the entrance, raising their swords in honor as the Kings and Queens entered Aslan's How.

The room stretched into darkness under a low ceiling supported by rows of columns. The flickering fires of the blacksmiths cast weird shadows as Dwarfs hammered away, making armor and weapons. Peter nodded approvingly at the preparations.

Susan called her older brother over to her. She was standing at the entrance to a long tunnel. We joined her in the tunnel, where ancient carvings decorated the walls. The mosaics illustrated scenes from Narnia's history. They showed a tall woman battling a young boy. There was another picture of two girls riding a giant Lion.

"What is this place?" Peter asked.

"You don't know?" I asked, surprised. I led them through the tunnel and lit a track of oil with my torch. The oil flared brightly, circling around a big, cathedral-like room with a high domed ceiling.

The Kings and Queens gasped when they saw the enormous stone table looming, broken, in the center of the room. They all recognized the powerful place where Aslan had sacrificed his life for them.

Lucy placed her hand on the cold stone. "Aslan must know what he's doing," she said, sounding uncertain. .

Peter put his arm around Lucy's shoulders. "I think it's up to us now," he said.

Chapter 4

I approached the edge of the wood where High Queen Susan was giving archery instructions to a group of Fauns and Satyrs. Trufflehunter helped by parading a dummy of a Telmarine soldier on a stick. The student archers loosed their arrows at the dummy. They all missed by a wide margin.

"Not a scratch," Trufflehunter announced, and the archers groaned.

I raised my own bow and shot the helmet clean off the dummy soldier.

"Not bad," Susan said.

"Well, I was trained by the finest archer in the Telmarine army," I replied.

Susan pointed at a pinecone far in the distance. Then she fitted an arrow onto her bow, drew back the string, and fired. The arrow sailed through the air and severed a tiny twig holding the pinecone.

We both watched it fall to the ground. It landed by the hoof of a horse. On the horse was a mounted Telmarine soldier—a real one—watching us.

Susan gasped, and loosed an arrow at the soldier, but he had already galloped off into the trees.

"We'd better tell the others," I said grimly.

Ten minutes later, we'd given our report to the Narnian War Council gathered around the cracked Stone Table.

Reepicheep twirled his whiskers with his fingers. "What do you propose we do, your Majesty?" he asked.

"We should start planning for—" I began.

But Peter replied at the same time.

Even though it bothered me to defer to Peter, I let the High King speak first. He had already led the Narnians to freedom once before.

"Miraz's men are coming," Peter continued. "That means those same men aren't protecting his castle."

"You want to attack the castle?" I asked in disbelief.

Queen Lucy sat down on one half of the Stone Table. "Why don't we wait here?" she suggested.

"Wait for what?" Peter argued. "We're outnumbered. They have better equipment. Our only hope is to strike them before they strike us."

"But nobody's ever taken the castle," I argued.

Peter gave me a smile that made me feel like a child. "Look, I appreciate what you've done here," he told me, "but this isn't a fortress, it's a tomb. We need to capture Miraz alive. If we control the King, we control the kingdom."

"He's not King yet!" I said.

Peter looked me right in the eyes. "But he soon will be if we don't do something about it."

I sighed. I couldn't argue with that.

Peter faced Glenstorm, the oldest Centaur. "If we can get your troops in, can you handle the guards?"

Glenstorm thumped his fist against his mighty chest. "Or die trying, my liege."

"That's what I'm worried about!" Lucy piped up. "You're

all acting like there are only two options—dying here or dying there! Have you forgotten who really freed Narnia, Peter?"

Peter took a deep breath and closed his hand around the pommel of his sword. "I think we've waited for Aslan long enough," he said. And with that it was decided—we would take back the castle.

Chapter 5

That night, flying Gryphons carried me, Peter, Edmund, Susan and Trumpkin to a tall tower of the castle. We knocked out the tower guards, and then left Edmund on the roof to signal our troops outside the gate when the drawbridge was down.

Directly below us was my tutor's chamber. We shimmied down a rope until we reached the balcony outside Cornelius's window. I rapped gently on the glass. There was no answer, so I forced the lock.

I eased myself inside. "Professor?" I whispered. His

books were scattered all around the room, and on the floor I found his wire-rimmed glasses. "I have to find him," I told Peter.

The High King shook his head. "You don't have time," he said. "The others are relying on you to get that gate open."

"Professor Cornelius kept the horn safe for decades," I argued. "You wouldn't be here without him, and neither would I."

Trumpkin put his hand on my arm. "I can handle the drawbridge alone," he offered.

I nodded at him gratefully. "I can still get to the gate by the time you find Miraz." When I saw Peter glance at Susan, both of them frowning uncertainly, I said, "Please. Cornelius is the closest thing to a father I've ever had."

"If anyone sees you . . . ," Peter warned.

"They won't," I promised.

I ran out of the room, heading for a back stairwell that I knew would have only a few guards. I had grown up in this castle—I knew how to get to the dungeons without being seen.

Cornelius was in a simple cell. He was shackled to the

wall, his tiny body curled up on a pallet of rags. I clamped my hand over his mouth. He awoke, startled, but relaxed when he saw me.

My tutor noticed my sword and armor. "I didn't help you escape just so you could break back in. You must get out before Miraz learns you're here."

I handed him back his wire-rimmed glasses. "He's going to learn soon enough," I said. "We're giving him your cell."

"You don't understand!" Cornelius insisted. "You are not the first Caspian to stand in the way of your uncle's ambition." He grabbed me by my shoulders. "Do not underestimate Miraz as your father did."

My stomach churned. "What are you talking about?" I asked. Could my uncle really have killed my father? It suddenly made sense, and I fought back tears as anger overwhelmed me. "Miraz . . ."

"I'm sorry," Cornelius said simply.

Furious, I fled the dungeon, running through secret corridors and back hallways, climbing through the castle until I reached the servants' quarters next to my uncle's bedchamber. I slipped through that room and opened a hidden door that led to where Miraz lay sleeping beside his

wife. In the corner was my nephew's crib.

I stood above my snoring uncle and drew my sword.

His eyes opened wide. "Oh, thank goodness," Miraz said. "You're safe."

"You're not," I replied. "Get up."

Miraz climbed out of bed, and I followed him with my sword.

"Stay where you are," I told my aunt.

Miraz examined my scowling face. "You know, some families might consider this inappropriate behavior."

I held the edge of the sword to my uncle's neck. "That didn't stop you."

Miraz smirked. "But you're not like me, are you?" he asked. "It's sad. The first time you've shown any backbone . . . and it's such a waste." He glanced behind me, and I stepped aside to look. My aunt had gotten out of bed and now held a loaded crossbow pointed at my back.

"Put the sword down, Caspian," Prunaprismia said. "I don't want to do this."

"I don't want you to, either," said Susan from behind me. She and Peter entered the chamber. Susan had an arrow aimed at my aunt.

"What are you doing?" Peter asked me angrily. "We need him alive!"

My sword shook in my hand. "First I want the truth," I said. I glared at my uncle. "Did you kill my father?"

"You said your brother died in his sleep!" Prunaprismia cried.

Miraz shrugged. "That was more or less true."

"How could you?" my aunt asked.

Miraz suddenly pressed his neck against the side of my sword. "You need to make a choice," he told my aunt. "Do you want our child to be King? Or do you want him to be fatherless like Caspian?" My sword cut into his flesh, and a trickle of blood seeped into his collar.

I stepped back, not sure what to do.

Susan shifted her aim toward Miraz. "Stay right there!" she ordered, but Miraz pressed himself against my sword again.

I lowered my weapon, and Peter rushed at Miraz.

"No!" Prunaprismia yelled. She pulled the crossbow trigger, and the bolt shot toward me, nicking my arm and spinning me backward.

Susan loosed her arrow, just missing Miraz's ear.

My uncle slammed the door shut behind him as he escaped. My aunt screamed, and her voice echoed like an alarm through the castle's corridors.

Chapter 6

Peter, Susan and I raced out of the castle into the courtyard. In front of me, I could see that Trumpkin and Reepicheep had succeeded—the gate was down. "Now, Ed!" Peter yelled.

Edmund signaled the Narnian troops to charge across the drawbridge. But my aunt's scream had lost us the element of surprise. Telmarine soldiers swarmed into the courtyard.

"Peter, it's too late!" Susan screamed. "We have to call it off!"

But Peter refused to listen.

The Narnian army clashed against the Telmarines. Fauns brought down their swords. Reepicheep's army fought fiercely. The Centaur Glenstorm led the main attack, battling the soldiers, but the Narnians were outnumbered.

Meanwhile, Miraz had retaken the gatehouse, and his men were closing the drawbridge again. Hundreds of Telmarine archers appeared on the castle balconies, taking aim at the Narnians below.

"Fall back!" Peter screamed. "We need to retreat! Now!"

I dashed toward the stable, hoping Cornelius would meet me there. Luckily, he was waiting for me with two saddled horses. He and I mounted one, and Peter jumped on the other. The Narnians were retreating through the rapidly closing gate. Glenstorm leaped across the moat with Susan riding on his back.

We charged up the angled drawbridge and launched off the top, barely making it across the moat. Around us, Reepicheep and the mice scrambled down the walls, and other beasts jumped into the water.

I glanced back and saw dozens of Narnians still fighting the Telmarines. They were trapped behind the gate. They

fought bravely, but I knew they were lost.

Edmund swooped low, riding on the back of a Gryphon.

Our battered army fled back to Aslan's How. It had been a terrible defeat.

Lucy met us at the entrance to the How with her crystal bottle of healing cordial in her hand. "What happened?" she asked.

Peter glared at me. "Ask *him*," he seethed. "If Caspian had stuck to the plan, those soldiers might be alive now."

"If we'd stayed here like I suggested," I shot back, "they *definitely* would be."

"*You* called *us*, remember?"

"My first mistake," I told him.

"No," Peter replied. "That was thinking you could lead these people. You invaded Narnia! You don't have any more right to lead it than Miraz does."

I was nothing like my uncle! I whipped out my sword and pointed it at Peter. He drew his own blade.

"Stop it!" Edmund shouted. He and Glenstorm hurried over, the Centaur carrying the limp body of Trumpkin. Glenstorm placed the red-haired Dwarf in front of Lucy.

Lucy poured a drop of her magic cordial onto Trumpkin's

lips. It was too late.

But suddenly the Dwarf coughed. And smiled. "My . . . dear little friend," Trumpkin whispered to Lucy. He sat up, a panicked look on his face. "Why are you all standing here? The Telmarines will be here soon!"

I strode into the underground hideout. I didn't feel like fighting Peter anymore. How had everything gone so wrong?

"Are you glad you used that magic horn now, boy?" Nikabrik asked with a sneer. The black-haired Dwarf followed me down a hallway decorated with images of the ancient royal family. "Your Kings and Queens failed us. Your army's half dead." He crept closer. "You want your uncle's throne? We can get it for you."

I didn't trust the Dwarf, but I wanted to prove myself and save Narnia. He pulled me by the arm to the Stone Table where two hooded figures waited. "There is a power so great," he said, "that it kept Aslan at bay for a hundred years."

The two figures leaned closer. One was a Wer-wolf and the other a hideous Hag. "What you hate, so will we," the Hag hissed. "No one hates better than us."

My head was reeling. "You can guarantee Miraz's death?"

"And more," the Hag promised. "Let the circle be drawn."

The Wer-wolf carved a ring in the dirt with his claw, and the Hag shook powder into the ring. Instantly, the room became icy cold. My breath billowed out in a frosted mist. The Hag pulled out a wand and stabbed it into the Stone Table. Icicles jagged out, filling the archway with a pane of shimmering ice. My breath wisped across the ice, forming patterns, darkening.

Something was terribly wrong.

The Wer-wolf held me down as I squirmed. "This isn't what I wanted!" I shouted. The Wer-wolf and the Hag were conjuring the White Witch! Nikabrik had always hated me— and now he'd tricked me!

"One drop of Adam's blood," the Hag said coldly, "and the power to rule Narnia will be ours again."

The Wer-wolf wrenched my hand up, and the Hag slashed it with her dagger. Blood welled along the cut. They shoved me toward the darkening ice.

"Stop!" Peter hollered.

The Wer-wolf and the Hag glared at Peter and Edmund in the doorway. The Wer-wolf leaped at Edmund, his fangs flashing, but Edmund stabbed him with his sword.

Nikabrik charged at Peter, but before he could reach him, Lucy stopped him with her dagger. "Don't even think about it," she threatened. Nikabrik raised his arm to strike Lucy, but then stiffened. Behind him, Trumpkin yanked his sword out of Nikabrik's back.

But the Hag wasn't finished with me. "Just one drop," she snarled as she reached for my bloody hand.

"Get away from him," Peter ordered, stalking closer.

The Hag smiled. "Peter, dear," she cooed, "you know you can't win this war alone. We can call a power greater than the Lion's."

Peter lowered his sword, considering the Hag's offer.

But suddenly Edmund jammed his sword into the pane of ice, shattering it. A terrifying screech filled the cave as the chunks of ice collapsed onto the ground.

Peter struck down the Hag. Then the High King slumped down next to me, both of us exhausted and ashamed at how close we'd come to bringing a great evil back to Narnia.

Chapter 7

Later, I sat on the cliff's edge atop the How, staring at the forest, wiping tears from my eyes. Cornelius found me there and sat beside me.

"They're right," I told him. "I'm no more fit to be King than Miraz."

Cornelius sighed. "Then I've failed you," he said. "Have you never wondered why I told you all the stories of Old Narnia?" He pulled back his hood. "Look at me. I'm not just short. My mother was a Dwarf. I've risked my life all these years so that you would know the Old Ways, so you might

be a better King than those before you."

"Why didn't you tell me about my father?" I asked.

"Because Narnia needs a just ruler," Cornelius replied, "not a vengeful one."

I picked at my bandaged hand, confused and ashamed.

"Everything I did," Cornelius continued, "was only because I believe in you. You have a chance to become the Telmarine who saved Narnia."

I stood up. The trees on the horizon appeared to be moving. I knew it was the soldiers, making their way through the forest.

I hurried down to the war room. Peter was there. He was suggesting that Lucy go out into the forest to find Aslan and reinforcements for the Narnian army. But there was little time.

Suddenly I had an idea. I could stall. "Miraz may be a tyrant and a murderer," I said, "but as King, he's subject to the traditions of his people. There is one tradition in particular that may buy us some time."

I explained that I would challenge Miraz to a duel. We would fight to the death, and the reward for the victor would be total surrender of the opposing army.

Edmund rode out to deliver the challenge, and he quickly returned with Miraz's acceptance. Miraz had no choice. The Telmarines would have seen his refusal to fight a boy half his age as cowardice.

There was one amendment to the duel. High King Peter insisted that *he* fight Miraz instead. Even as Peter prepared to enter the combat ring, I tried to change his mind. "This is *my* fight," I insisted.

"We tried that already," Peter snapped. But he softened when he saw my miserable expression. "Look," he explained, "if there's ever to be peace with the Telmarines, you've got to be the one to bring it. If I don't make it . . . Narnia's future is in your hands."

Edmund handed Peter his helmet. "It's time," he said.

Peter strode out into the combat ring that had been set up outside Aslan's How. Ignoring the cheers of the thousands of Narnian and Telmarine soldiers outside, I helped Lucy and Susan prepare for their journey.

In an area of the tunnels used as stables, I gave Lucy a boost onto my horse. "Destrier has always served me well," I told her. "You're in good hands."

"Or hooves," Lucy joked.

Before I could help Susan, she mounted Destrier herself. "Good luck," I said.

"Thanks," she replied in a chilly voice.

I knew she was still furious at the way I'd handled myself with Miraz and Nikabrik. I couldn't blame her. I was angry with myself, too, for being tricked by the hateful Dwarf. "Maybe it's time you took this back," I said. I held up her ivory horn.

Her face softened slightly. "Why don't you hold on to it?" she said. "You might need to call me again."

I nodded, and put the horn back in my belt.

Susan tugged the reins, and Destrier carried the two Queens out of the tunnel.

Chapter 8

Not long after Susan and Lucy left, a terrible feeling came over me. Something was not right. I jumped onto a horse and followed them.

Only a short distance into the forest, I found Susan surrounded by Telmarine soldiers. Lucy and Destrier were disappearing on the horizon at a gallop. As I rushed toward Susan, she shot one of the soldiers with an arrow, but she couldn't handle them all.

I dashed between her and a swordsman, parrying a blow

with my own blade. As Susan stared up at me, amazed, I offered her my hand.

"You sure you don't need that horn?" I asked.

Susan swung up behind me on the horse, and we hurtled back toward Aslan's How.

The battle in the combat ring was already underway by the time we dismounted next to Edmund. Peter saw us and took a break to come over. He was already in pain, holding his shoulder. Miraz was hurt, too, though.

"Lucy?" he asked.

"She got through," Susan replied. She smiled at me. "With a little help."

"Thanks," Peter told me, and I nodded. Then Peter glanced toward the top of the How where other archers were stationed. "You'd better get up there," he said to Susan. "Just in case."

Susan gave her brother a quick hug, and he yelped in pain, grabbing his shoulder again.

"Keep smiling," Edmund whispered to Peter.

Peter gritted his teeth and raised his sword to the Narnians, who erupted in cheers for their champion. I helped Edmund tie Peter's shield onto his wounded arm

before pushing him back out into the ring.

The battle between Peter and Miraz turned nasty. Miraz pounded away at Peter's bad arm. The shield held, but the blows had to hurt terribly. Peter was faster and younger than my uncle and began to gain the advantage. After many rounds of fighting, Miraz, exhausted, left himself open, and Peter struck him across the ribs. Miraz's sword went flying, and my uncle dropped to his knees.

Peter stared down at Miraz.

"What's the matter, boy?" Miraz demanded. "Too cowardly to take a life?"

Peter paused a moment before turning to look at me. "It's not mine to take," he said. Then he kicked Miraz's sword toward me.

I picked it up, shocked. Everyone fell silent as I entered the ring and Peter limped to the sidelines. I stared down at my uncle, the sword heavy in my hands.

Miraz gave me a sickly smile. "Perhaps you *do* have the makings of a Telmarine King after all."

I raised his sword . . . and smashed it down into the dirt.

"Not a King like you," I spat at him. "Keep your life, but

I'm giving the Narnians back their Kingdom."

Susan and the other archers waved down to me from the top of the How as Lord Sopespian rushed into the ring toward Miraz.

I strode back toward Peter. Out of the corner of my eye, too quickly for the crowd to see, I glimpsed Lord Sopespian stabbing Miraz in the back with an arrow. He immediately pointed up at Susan and the other archers. "Treachery!" he screamed to the Telmarine soldiers. "They shot him! They murdered our King!" He rushed at Peter with his sword raised as the enraged crowd erupted in battle.

"Peter!" I screamed out in warning.

"Be ready!" Peter called back to me, defending himself from Sopespian's sword attack. Glenstorm appeared beside me with a horse. "Go now!"

I leaped onto the horse, and Glenstorm and I galloped toward the entrance to the How.

The war had begun.

Chapter 9

Glenstorm and I rushed down the ramp, and we took a quick turn down a long chamber where a group of Narnian soldiers waited for us.

The ceiling shuddered. The Telmarines were using their catapults, I was sure of it.

Underground, I turned my horse in front of our gathered soldiers. I had a plan. "Narnians, charge!" I shouted, and then I led them through the subterranean chamber at full speed.

Slowly I counted to ten as we barreled through the

dark space. When I hit ten, I gave a signal, and my soldiers knocked down the pillars holding up the ceiling. Without their support, the earthen roof collapsed behind us as we dashed through the chamber.

Our ceiling was the ground beneath the Telmarine cavalry. When it fell, so did their army. Screams echoed behind us as their horsemen plummeted into darkness. Some of the Telmarines were injured in the fall, and the rest were easy targets for our archers.

At the end of the underground hollow, I led the Narnian riders up a ramp. We emerged behind the remainder of the Telmarine cavalry, surrounding them. Edmund raced up, leading a group of Centaur archers, who launched arrows at the front lines of the enemy. It looked as though the battle had swung in our favor.

But then the Telmarine generals sent in their infantry. Five thousand soldiers marched toward us. We had less than a fifth of that number.

Our Gryphons swooped at them, carrying archers in their talons. But the Telmarines had giant crossbows that shot our Gryphons right out of the sky.

"Back to the How!" Peter shouted across the battlefield.

But before we could reach the safety of our hideout, the Telmarine catapults blocked the How's entrance with boulders.

We crouched down in front of the How, fighting one on one. I saw Edmund wielding two swords as he swung at the enemy. Reepicheep and his band of mice slew surprised Telmarines with their rapiers. Ahead of me, a group of Minotaurs were defeated by the giant crossbows, and our mightiest Giant fell prey to the same weapons. As I battled, I glimpsed Trufflehunter fighting fiercely with his sharp claws, and I heard Glenstorm crying out over his fallen son.

Finally, I was pushed up against the edge of the collapsed hole beside Peter, Edmund and Trumpkin, until all of us were knocked down into the pit. At the bottom we scrambled to our feet, defending ourselves from the Telmarines who had jumped down after us.

Just as General Glozelle was about to spear me with his pike, the earthen ceiling above him rippled. Tree roots exploded from the ground and reached down to grab the soldier, wrenching him up into the ceiling.

We climbed out of the pit to see what was going on.

The entire tree line of the forest came forward, churning the earth.

Edmund and Peter glanced at each other and smiled. "Lucy," they said together.

Queen Lucy had brought reinforcements—the awakened trees of Narnia!

Telmarines scrambled in retreat as roots erupted out of the ground, entangling them. Green shoots burst up around the giant crossbows. A grove of oaks hurled acorns at the infantry, and wherever the seeds landed, new trees sprouted, encircling the Telmarines.

Peter raised his sword and led the Narnians in a triumphant charge.

"Back to the castle!" the Telmarine generals screamed.

We ran along with the frontline of the forest, watching as the Telmarines raced toward the river, its bridge now clogged with cavalry. Halfway across the bridge, the Telmarines stopped suddenly. Waiting for them on the other shore was an enormous golden Lion.

Aslan.

Lucy stepped out from behind him.

One Telmarine general raised his sword, spurred his

horse, and charged at Aslan.

In response, Aslan let out a deafening roar that rippled the river. The water receded from the bank and sucked upstream in a violent whirlpool. The liquid swirled and solidified until it took the shape of a towering man. It was the God of the River, with rushing water for a beard.

The Telmarines screamed as the River God churned downstream, tossing soldiers aside like twigs. The God grabbed the bridge, which was still jammed with cavalry, and ripped it up from its foundations. He crushed it into splinters.

Finally, the River God crashed back into the riverbed, washing what was left of the Telmarine army away in a massive wave.

Then the river settled, calm and sparkling in the sunlight.

Chapter 10

I waded across the river with the surviving Narnians, joining Lucy, Peter, Susan and Edmund beside Aslan. We kneeled before the Lion.

"Rise, Kings and Queens of Narnia," Aslan said.

Peter, Susan, Edmund and Lucy rose to their feet.

"Including you," Aslan told me.

I looked up at him, surprised. "I don't think I'm ready," I said.

Aslan nodded. "It's for that very reason I know you are."

Peter pulled me up beside him as the crowd cheered our victory.

Later that evening, all the Narnians celebrated in the castle's main hall, toasting the newly crowned King. Me. I was surprised at how heavily the crown sat on my brow and how nervous I felt wearing it.

Outside, the Narnians and the remaining Telmarines gathered on the edge of a cliff outside the castle walls. Aslan stood under a big oak tree next to Peter, Susan, Edmund and Lucy. Next to me were Cornelius, Trumpkin and Trufflehunter, all wearing their new official robes.

I faced the crowd. "Narnia belongs to the Narnians just as it does to Man," I began. "Any Telmarines who wish to stay and live in peace are welcome to do so. For those of you who feel you cannot, Aslan will return you to the home of our forefathers."

One of the Telmarines stepped forward. "But it's been generations since we left Telmar," he said.

"We're not referring to Telmar," Aslan replied. "Your ancestors were seafaring brigands run aground on an island where they found a cave—a rare chasm that brought them here from their world. They came from the same

world as our Kings and Queens."

"I'll go," Glozelle called out.

Prunaprismia walked out of the crowd, holding her son. "So will we," she said.

"Because you have spoken first, your future in that world shall be good," Aslan told them. He turned toward the oak tree, which suddenly split at its roots. The crack traveled up the trunk, forming an arched doorway.

"We'll go, too," Peter announced. "Come on," he said to his brother and sisters. "Our time's up." He unstrapped his glorious sword and held it out to me and smiled. "We're not needed here anymore."

I took the sword gratefully. "I will hold it until your return," I vowed.

"But we're not coming back," Susan said sadly.

Lucy gasped. "We're not?"

"You and Ed are," Peter added quickly. "At least, I think Aslan means for you to return."

"Why?" Lucy asked the Lion. "Did Susan and Peter do something wrong?"

"Quite the opposite, dear one," Aslan answered. "Your brother and sister have learned what they can from this

world. Now it's time for them to live in their own."

"It's all right," Peter told Lucy. He glanced up at the castle and smiled sadly. "One day you'll see." He took his little sister's hand. "Come on."

With a final glance back, Susan stepped into the archway of the oak tree, and the old Kings and Queens once again departed our world.

I turned to face my friends and subjects, truly ready to rule the beautiful and wondrous land of Narnia. I was the new King.

My adventure was just beginning.